W9-CCJ-334

MOUSE'S
FIRST DAY OF
SCHOOL

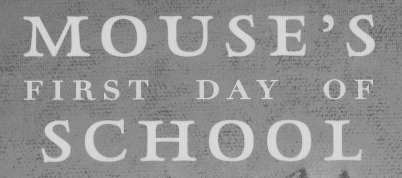

Lauren Thompson

Illustrated by

Buket Erdogan

SIMON & SCHUSTER BOOKS FOR YOUNG READERS

New York   London   Toronto   Sydney   Singapore

To Owen and Graham, best-of-all buddies—L. T.

To Kevin and Alyssa, for all the fun and inspiration—B. E.

SIMON & SCHUSTER BOOKS FOR YOUNG READERS
An imprint of Simon & Schuster Children's Publishing Division
1230 Avenue of the Americas, New York, New York 10020
Text copyright © 2003 by Lauren Thompson
Illustrations copyright © 2003 by Buket Erdogan
SIMON & SCHUSTER BOOKS FOR YOUNG READERS is a trademark of Simon & Schuster.
Book design by Paula Winicur
Manufactured in China
10 9 8 7 6 5 4 3 2 1
Library of Congress Card Number: 2002036489
ISBN 0-689-84727-0

One bright morning,
Mouse found a hiding place...

that took him to a
brand new space.

Down on the floor,
Mouse found . . .
one,
  two,
    three,
      four
        blocks!

Vrim,
vrum,
vroom

a car!

Up on the shelf,
Mouse found . . .

A, B, C
books!

Blinky, cuddly, curly dolls!

Viny, climby, twiny plants!

Over on the table,
Mouse found...

red,

yellow,

blue

paint!

Squiggle,

scribble,

dot

crayons!

snacks!

There in the corner,
Mouse found . . .

circle,

triangle,

square

puzzles!

Feathery,
floppy,
boppy
hats!

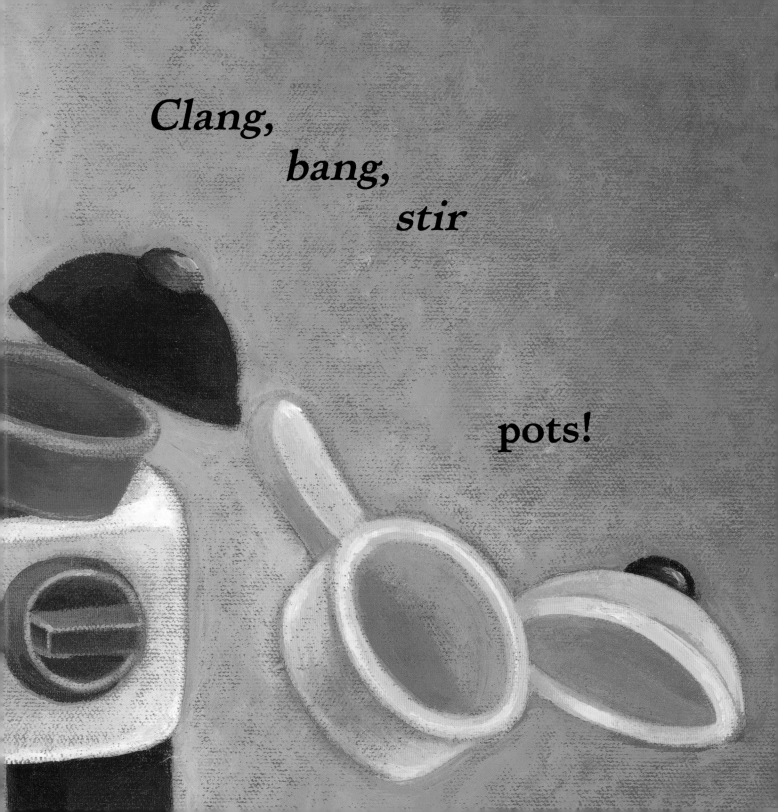

Clang,

bang,

stir

pots!

Then all around,
Mouse found...

Wiggly, giggly,
best of all
friends!

Welcome to school, Mouse!